# Animal

# The lion and the mouse

Lion said, "Look here, Mouse.

I want something to eat.

I will eat you."

"Please don't eat me," said Mouse.
"Let me go, Lion.
Let me go, and
I will do something for you."

Lion said, "You can't help me, Mouse.
You are too little."

"Yes, I am little," said Mouse.
But I am not too little to help you.
Let me go, and you will see."

Lion said, "I will let you go,
but what will you do for me, Mouse?"

"I will surprise you," said Mouse.
"You will see what I can do."

Lion shouted, "Run fast, Mouse.
Run fast."
Mouse ran away.

"Help! Help!" said Lion.
"I want to get away from here,
but I can't. What can I do?
Where are some big animals
to help me? I can't see Elephant.
I can't see Goat, or Fox."

Mouse said, "**I** am here, Lion.
I will help you get away."

Lion said, "**You** can't help me.
You are too little."

Mouse said, "No, Lion.
I am not too little to help you.
I can help you get away."

"Do something fast," said Lion.

"A man will come and get me.

He will get you, too."

Mouse said, "Look, Lion. See what I can do."

"You **did** help me!" said Lion.
"You are little, Mouse,
but you did something for me."

"Yes, I did," said Mouse.
"But you did not eat me, Lion.
You did something for me, too."

# The Gingerbread Boy

The Little Old Woman said
to the Little Old Man,
"We want a little boy."

"Can you make a gingerbread boy?"
said the Little Old Man.

"Yes, I can," said the Little Old Woman.
"I can make a little gingerbread boy,"

The Little Old Woman did.

Gingerbread Boy wanted to play.
He didn't want to be with the
Little Old Woman and
the Little Old Man.
So he ran away.
The Little Old Woman shouted,
"Stop! Stop, Gingerbread Boy!"

The Little Old Man shouted,
"Come here, Gingerbread Boy."

"No!" said Gingerbread Boy.
"I don't want to be with you."

Gingerbread Boy ran away
from the Little Old Man.
He ran and ran.

Big Dog said, "Stop! Stop!
Come here, Gingerbread Boy."

Gingerbread Boy said, "No, Big Dog.
You want to eat me.
I ran away from the Little Old Man and
the Little Old Woman.
I will run away from you, too."

And Gingerbread Boy did.

Little Goat said, "Stop! Stop!
Come here, Gingerbread Boy."

Gingerbread Boy said, "No, Little Goat.

You want to eat me.

I ran away from the Little Old Man and

the Little Old Woman.

I ran away from Big Dog.

I will run away from you, too."

And Gingerbread Boy did.

Fox said, "Stop! Stop!
You can't swim, but I can.
I will swim, and let you ride.
Come here, Gingerbread Boy.
Let me help you."

And Gingerbread Boy did.

Fox said, "Here we are,
Gingerbread Boy.
You ran away from the Little Old Man
and the Little Old Woman.
You ran away from Big Dog,
and Little Goat.
But you can't run away from me!
I will eat you!"

And Fox did.